LiVi & GRACE

love your uniqueness
XO, Jenn

For my Olivia and Grace, so different and so loved. You are my happiness. —J. L.

For Ruby. Your smile lights up my world, and your heart is filled with sparkles, glitter, and a million unicorns. —M. J.

Livi & Grace

BY *Jennifer Lynch*

ILLUSTRATED BY *Missi Jay*

GREENLEAF
BOOK GROUP PRESS
www.gbgpress.com

Livi and Grace are sisters, in their hearts and in their name,
But they think it's odd when people feel they ought to be the same.
For when they are together and you see them face-to-face,
Livi looks and acts and plays the opposite of Grace.

When people ask, "You're sisters?" well, of course, they nod and grin,
And then explain they're different on the outside and within.

Each of them is special—her own self in heart and mind.
Each treasures her uniqueness and her sister's different kind.

Liv is neat and tidy, with perfectly styled hair.
Grace is wild and playful, and she overflows with flair.

Liv wears classic dresses; tights and flats are to her taste.
Grace wears lots of leopard print and leaves her boots unlaced.

The girls are both creative. Each has a special style,
And they love to dream up projects that they take on with a smile.

Livi draws and sketches and makes art that's realistic.
Grace sprays and spatters things; her work's expressionistic.

Livi wears her coat and boots when it's raining, you can bet,
But Grace will leave without them, calling, "Livi, come get wet!"

Then, when the clouds have parted, Grace will set off at a run,
Calling, "Livi, come explore with me! Let's go and get some sun."

The sisters ride their bikes to town for treats they want to buy.
Livi rings her silver bell while Grace's streamers fly.

Liv holds the handles carefully, while pedaling just right.
Grace swings her feet up in the air, shoes flashing pink and white.

Livi loves to eat with chopsticks and to sip her jasmine tea,
But Grace just pokes her sushi and says, "This stuff's not for me!"

While Livi tries all kinds of foods, proclaiming, "This is great!"
Grace would rather see familiar dinners on her plate.

When Grace zooms in on roller skates, Liv cries, "C'mon, Grace, stop!
It's time to serve the tea now; don't make me spill a drop."

Grace rolls her eyes—*whatever*—and scrunches up her face,
While Livi smooths her napkin and politely takes her place.

At school, where Liv is quiet, Grace will always raise her hand.

Livi's happiest in reading; Grace's favorite class is band.

Liv likes sitting quietly with friends in study hall,

But Grace likes gym and teamwork and long games of volleyball.

At noon they race each other to their favorite playground things.
For Grace, it is the curvy slide; for Livi, it's the swings.

A boy who sees them racing asks, "Hey, which of you just won?"
They answer, "Winning's not the point. We both are having fun!"

Livi and Grace are sisters—best friends, some folks would say.
They know that they are different, and they're happiest that way.

Livi loves that Grace is filled with spirit, verve, and light,
While Grace loves Livi's kindess, how she's elegant and polite.

One night they sit beside a tent and gaze up at the sky.
Liv feels a sense of magic, but she doesn't know quite why.

Grace murmurs, "Stars are beautiful, like tiny flicks of flame."
Livi answers, "There are billions, and no two are just the same!"

These sisters know a secret that they'd like to share with you:
Differences are interesting—and life-enriching, too.
Appreciate what's special about everyone you know,
And love what makes YOU special, from head to tippy-toe.

Our differences are beautiful—they're blessings through and through.
There's no one way that's best to be, so be the you that's you!
You're perfect, good, and lovable—yes, just the way you are,
And everyone is special: everyone's a star.

Dear friend,

You are lovely just the way you are. Don't compare yourself to anyone else. Don't pretend to be anyone else — be proud, be true. Be You!

Love your uniqueness!

Hugs,
Livi

you are good

With thanks to
Simone Kaplan of Picture Book People, Inc., for her expert editorial direction,
and to Rebecca Kai Dotlich, for helping get the rhyme and rhythm right!

Distributed by Greenleaf Book Group

For ordering information or special discounts for bulk purchases, please contact Greenleaf Book Group at
PO Box 91869, Austin, TX 78709, 512.891.6100.

Design and art direction by Stephanie Bart-Horvath • Cover design by Stephanie Bart-Horvath
Illustrations and hand lettering by Missi Jay

Publisher's Cataloging-in-Publication data is available.

Print ISBN: 978-1-62634-591-1 • eBook ISBN: 978-1-62634-592-8

Printed in the United States of America on acid-free paper
19 20 21 22 23 24   10 9 8 7 6 5 4 3 2 1
First Edition